The Pony-Crazed Princess

A Surprise for Princess Ellie

"Let's go for a picnic ride," suggested Ellie. "I'll take Starlight." She knew she'd be less likely to worry about the bay mare if she could see her all the time.

"That's not a good idea," said Meg.

Ellie looked at Meg in surprise. What was the matter with Starlight? she wondered. And why was Meg being so secretive about it?

The Pony-Crazed Princess

A Surprise for Princess Ellie

Diana Kimpton

Illustrated by Lizzie Finlay

USBORNE

For Caitlin

This edition first published in 2014 by Usborne Publishing Ltd.,
Usborne House, 83-85 Saffron Hill, London EC1N 8RT, England.
www.usborne.com

First published in 2004. Based on an original concept by Anne Finnis.
Text copyright © 2004 by Diana Kimpton and Anne Finnis.

Illustrations copyright © 2004 by Lizzie Finlay.

A CIP catalogue record for this book is available from the British Library.
This edition published in America in 2015 AE.
PB ISBN 9780794534325 ALB ISBN 9781601303608
JFMAM JASOND/16 01428/10
Printed in China.

Chapter 1

"Good girl," said Princess Ellie, as she
cantered Moonbeam toward the last jump.
The palomino pony eyed the wooden poles
warily and tried to swerve away. But Ellie
was ready for her. She kept a firm hold on
the reins and pushed the pony on with her
legs. Moonbeam did as she was told. She
leaped forward and cleared the jump easily.

The Pony-Crazed Princess

Ellie galloped between the finishing posts and pulled her pony to a halt. Then she turned around to see how the others were doing.  She was just in time to watch her best friend soar over the wooden poles on Rainbow. Kate's jumping had improved enormously since she came to live with her gran, the palace cook. Maybe it was from all the practice she had on Ellie's ponies.

Prince John was further back, riding Sundance. The chestnut pony jumped over a fallen tree trunk and cantered down the hill towards the last obstacle. Then he pricked his ears forward, lifted his front legs

A Surprise for Princess Ellie

and bounded over it. Prince John grinned
broadly. It was hard to tell which of them
was enjoying themselves most, as they
galloped through the finish line.

"That was fantastic," said
John, as they rode slowly
back toward the stables.
"I'm going to ask my father
to build a cross-country
course in the grounds of
our palace – but I'm sure mine
will be longer."

"Of course it will," sighed Ellie. She really
liked John. He was the only royal person she
knew who shared her love of ponies. But he
did have an annoying habit of insisting
everything was bigger and better at his
home in Andirovia.

The Pony-Crazed Princess

Kate leaned forward and patted Rainbow's gray neck. "I'm not surprised you want one," she said. "Cross-country's much more exciting than jumping in the paddock."

"But even that's not as exciting as a real adventure," said John. "Do you remember how we went hunting for ghosts last time I came to stay?"

"I was really scared," said Ellie.

"So was I," agreed Kate.

A Surprise for Princess Ellie

"But it was still fun," laughed John. "What are we going to look for this time?" The girls stared at him blankly. "Well, aren't there any mysterious legends about your palace? What about tales of hidden treasure?"

"I've never heard any," said Ellie.

"Dragon's eggs?" asked John.

"Now you're being silly," giggled Kate.

"How about a secret passage, then?" suggested John. "All the *best* palaces have one of those. Our one at home is fantastic."

"But that's not secret," Ellie declared with delight. "It can't be if *you* know about it."

At that moment, they reached the lane that led to the palace stables. A bay pony

whinnied loudly and cantered across the
nearby field to meet them. She was larger
than the ponies they were riding, and the
long hair that nearly hid her hooves made
her look like a miniature cart horse. She
skidded to a halt beside the fence and put
her head over the top rail.

"This is Starlight," explained Ellie, as
Moonbeam sniffed noses with the bay
pony. "Do you like her?"

A Surprise for Princess Ellie

"She's great," said John. It was the first time he had come to stay since Starlight arrived, so he hadn't met her before. "She looks much better than she did in that photo you emailed to me."

Ellie smiled proudly. "I'd only just found her then. She'd been living wild for so long that she looked really neglected."

"She doesn't anymore," said John. He twisted a finger thoughtfully in Sundance's chestnut mane and added, "She's quite fat now."

"No, she's not," said Ellie, indignantly. "She's just well built. Ponies like her have big bones." She turned Moonbeam firmly away from the fence and led the way toward the stable yard. "You don't have to be thin to be beautiful."

The Pony-Crazed Princess

There was a long, awkward pause. Then
Kate broke the silence by saying, "Wasn't
Ellie clever to catch Starlight?" She looked
wistful for a moment and added, "I wish
I could find a pony."

"So do I," said John. "I'd like a palomino,
like Moonbeam."

"Copycat!" cried Ellie.

"No, I'm not," said John. "My palomino
would be bigger than yours."

"Then it wouldn't be like Moonbeam,
would it?" Ellie declared. "Anyway, you
don't need another pony. You've got two
already." She'd seen plenty of pictures of
the beautiful, chestnut mares he'd left
behind in Andirovia.

"Why shouldn't I have three?" argued
John. "*You* already had Sundance,

A Surprise for Princess Ellie

Moonbeam, Rainbow *and* Shadow when you got Starlight. That's five." He sighed and shrugged his shoulders. "Anyway, there's no point arguing about it. My father already thinks I spend too much time riding. There's no way he'd buy me another pony."

"My dad won't get me a pony at all," added Kate, very quietly.

The sadness in her voice made Ellie feel guilty. It was mean of her to argue with John about how many ponies they had, when Kate didn't even have one. Ellie was happy to share her ponies with her best friend, but she knew that wasn't the same. Kate desperately wanted a pony of her own. If only there was something Ellie could do to help.

Chapter 2

The stable yard was deserted when Ellie, John and Kate rode in. There was no sign of Meg, the palace groom, but she had left the ponies' stalls ready for them. Each one had a thick bed of sweet-smelling straw, a bulging haynet and a bucket of clean water. They led the ponies inside, took off their saddles and bridles, and brushed their

A Surprise for Princess Ellie

backs carefully. Then they left them
to have a well-earned rest.

Ellie was just rinsing
Moonbeam's bit under
the faucet when Shadow,
her black Shetland, trotted
into the stable yard.
He was pulling his
carriage with Great
Aunt Edwina in the
driving seat, and he
looked very proud of himself.
He carried his head high as his tiny
hooves clattered on the cobbles.

Great Aunt Edwina pulled him to a halt
and announced, "That was a wonderful
drive. We went all the way around the deer
park, just as I used to when I was a girl."

She waited while Kate ran over and took hold of Shadow's bridle. Then she climbed slowly to the ground, her long skirt rustling as she moved. "I expect you children are looking forward to the party tomorrow."

"That's why my family has come to stay," said John. "We didn't want to miss it. Although, I'm sure it won't be as grand as our parties in Andirovia."

"Yes it will!" declared Ellie. "It's going to be great. There'll be music and dancing and jugglers and conjurers and everything."

"And I'm going too," cried Kate, her voice bouncing with enthusiasm. She wasn't usually allowed to attend royal events.

"Imagine your parents having their crystal jubilee," sighed Great Aunt Edwina. "I can't believe it's been fifteen years since they

A Surprise for Princess Ellie

became King and Queen. It seems like only yesterday. Time goes so much faster now than it did when I was a girl."

John sidled up to Ellie and nudged her hard in the ribs. "Ask her about the secret passage," he whispered. "She's so old, she might know."

"I might be old, but I am not deaf," said Great Aunt Edwina, sternly. "Why don't you ask me yourself?"

John's ears turned pink with embarrassment. He bowed politely and explained, "We were just wondering whether there's a secret passage in the palace. We have a wonderful one in ours."

The Pony-Crazed Princess

To Ellie's delight, her great aunt immediately replied, "That's not very secret, is it? It can't be if *you* know about it." John's ears grew even pinker as the old lady continued, "Now *our* passage really is secret. I searched and searched for it when I was a girl, but I never found it."

"So how do you know it's there?" asked Ellie, with a shiver of excitement. What if John was right? Maybe they could have an adventure.

"I read about it in my history books," explained Great Aunt Edwina. "It's called the Angel Pathway. Old King Liam had it built to

A Surprise for Princess Ellie

help him escape from danger, but he never told anyone else where it was." The old lady walked up to the black Shetland pony, stroked his nose and gave him his favorite treat – a peppermint. Then she waved goodbye and headed back toward the palace.

John waited until she was safely out of earshot. "I told you there'd be a secret passage," he said, with a triumphant grin.

Ellie grinned back. "Okay! You win! Now stop gloating and help me unharness Shadow."

She bent down and unhooked the long leather straps that attached the Shetland to the carriage. Then she and John slid the shafts out of the leather loops on either side of his harness.

The Pony-Crazed Princess

"I'll see to him now," called Kate, as she led the Shetland into his stall.

Ellie stepped forward to help, but changed her mind. Maybe it would be better to let Kate do it by herself. Then she could pretend Shadow was hers if she wanted to. It might make her feel better about not having a pony of her own.

Just then, Meg led Starlight into the stable yard. Ellie looked carefully at the bay mare. Maybe her tummy did stick out a little farther than it used to. But that still didn't mean that John was right. "Starlight's not fat, is she?" asked Ellie, hoping Meg would agree with her.

But she didn't. Instead, Meg sighed and ran her hand over the pony's bulging side. "She is getting a little big in the belly."

"I told you so," said John.

Ellie ignored him. She was more concerned with Starlight. "Does that matter?" she asked.

"I don't think so," replied Meg. "But just in case, I'll ask the vet to look at her next time he comes."

The mention of the vet threw Ellie into a panic. Suppose he found there was something horribly wrong with Starlight? Ellie couldn't bear the thought of anything happening to her newest pony.

Chapter 3

Ellie was very quiet as she walked back to the palace with John and Kate. "I'm worried about Starlight," she explained, when they asked what she was thinking about.

"We all are," said Kate. "I wish there was something we could do for her. But we've just got to wait for the vet."

"And he's not coming till after the party,"

added John. "So let's forget about it for now. We've got a secret passage to find."

Ellie smiled. For once, she was willing to admit that he was right. Searching for the Angel Pathway was just what she needed to keep her mind off Starlight's health. "When should we start?" she asked.

"Now," said John. "There's just enough time before supper."

Kate shook her head. "I can't. Dad's calling later, and I don't want to miss him." Her parents worked overseas and moved around a lot, while she stayed with her grandparents at the palace. It saved her from having to keep changing schools.

"Then it's just the two of us," said John. "But we'd better get changed for supper before we start."

A Surprise for Princess Ellie

Ellie waved goodbye to Kate and raced up the spiral staircase to her very pink bedroom. As soon as she was inside, she tore off her smelly riding clothes and replaced them with a much less comfortable pink dress with silver bows and matching silver sandals. Then she gave her face a quick wash, traded her everyday crown for her second-best tiara, and ran downstairs again.

John was already there, but before he had time to say anything Miss Stringle bustled into view. "I've been looking everywhere for you, Princess Aurelia."

Ellie groaned. She hated being called

by her real name and she suspected the arrival of her governess would upset their plans. Miss Stringle had strict ideas on how princesses should behave and she certainly wouldn't approve of searching for secret passages.

Miss Stringle ignored Ellie's reaction and curtseyed to John. "I've just been talking to your parents, Your Highness. The Emperor and Empress have agreed that you can help Princess Aurelia give everyone a surprise at tomorrow's celebration."

"Are we going to jump out of the cake?" cried Ellie. She'd seen someone do that once on television, and it looked enormously fun.

"Absolutely not," said her governess in a horrified voice. "That's far too undignified for a prince and princess. You are going to

A Surprise for Princess Ellie

sing a delightful song together. Now come to the schoolroom quickly. You must start practicing at once."

The song was better than Ellie expected. It had a bouncy tune and the words were easy to learn. "Can Kate join in too?" she asked. "It would sound much better with three of us."

"Of course she can't," said Miss Stringle. "This is a royal surprise and Kate is *not* royal."

Ellie scowled. She hated it when her governess looked down on Kate. "But she's my friend," argued Ellie.

"And mine," added John.

"That makes no difference," said Miss Stringle, firmly. "She is only the cook's granddaughter and she is not taking part."

Her attitude took the bounce out of their

singing and made the rest of the rehearsal drag slowly past. Ellie found it hard to concentrate. When she wasn't worrying about Starlight, she was worrying about Kate. It seemed so unfair that she should be left out of the performance, when she already had to put up with not seeing her parents and not having a pony.

Dinnertime dragged past just as slowly. Ellie and John wanted to finish as quickly as possible, so they could start hunting for the Angel Pathway. But the King and Queen were obviously not in a hurry and neither were John's parents. Ellie had never seen four people eat so slowly. They nibbled their smoked salmon and dilly-dallied with their roast turkey. Then they lingered over their strawberry meringue

A Surprise for Princess Ellie

gateau, deep in a really boring conversation.

Ellie swallowed the last of her meringue
and waited impatiently for them to stop
talking. So did John. He fidgeted from side
to side and drummed his feet
on the legs of his chair.
Then he picked up
a silver spoon and
tried to balance
it on his nose.
Ellie stifled a
giggle, licked her finger and
began to run it around and around the rim of
her crystal glass. The glass started to sing – a
single, high-pitched note that grew louder as
she moved her finger faster and faster.

"Aurelia!" hissed the Queen. "That is no
way to behave."

"Neither is that," groaned the Emperor, staring at the spoon that was now hanging from the end of John's nose.

"You'd better get down from the table, Aurelia," sighed the King. "Take John with you and find something sensible to do."

"But, please, make it nothing to do with ponies," said the Emperor. He was irritated by John's pony-craziness. He would prefer his son to like boats.

Ellie and John left the room as swiftly as they could. "Let's start the search up here," said John, leading the way up a narrow staircase to the next floor.

"What exactly are we looking for?" asked Ellie.

"Hollow walls, secret levers, that sort of thing," said John. He turned left into a

A Surprise for Princess Ellie

corridor and pointed at the wooden panels that lined the walls. "I bet the passage is somewhere behind that." He started to walk along the wall, knocking on the wood. "The part with the secret door will sound different."

Ellie followed his example. She worked her way along the opposite wall, without success. Every knock sounded as dull and uninteresting as all the others. There was no sign of anything unusual until they reached the landing. From there, a large, impressive staircase curved its

way down to the main entrance hall. The top
of the banister ended in a carved wooden
post, and the top of the post was decorated
with a glittering, golden ball.

"That looks like a giant
doorknob," cried Ellie. She
grabbed hold of it with both hands and tried
to turn it. The ball moved very slightly. She
tried again, heaving it around with all her
strength. This time the ball turned.

A Surprise for Princess Ellie

"Keep going," said John. "It's sure to open a secret door."

But it didn't. As Ellie twisted the ball around and around, it gradually unscrewed itself from the top of the post. Suddenly, it came free and wobbled sideways out of her fingers. She tried to grab it, but she was too late. The golden ball fell to the ground and rolled rapidly down the stairs, glittering in the light from the chandelier, as it thudded from step to step. Ellie and John raced after it, but the ball was going too fast. It reached the bottom before they did, and trundled to a halt in front of four pairs of feet.

The Pony-Crazed Princess

"Oh, no," groaned Ellie. The feet belonged to the King and Queen, and the Emperor and Empress of Andirovia. This time she really was in trouble.

Chapter 4

The King and Queen stared at the golden ball in surprise. So did the Emperor and Empress. Ellie's mind raced, wondering how she could talk her way out of this.

"Ouch!" cried the King, as he tried to kick the extremely hard ball out of his way. "What is the meaning of this, Aurelia?"

"I…um…we…uh…" For once, Ellie was

completely lost for words.

Luckily, John wasn't. "I'm very sorry. It was entirely my idea." He fluttered his eyelashes at his parents in an expression of complete innocence. "You asked us to play

something that had nothing to do with ponies. So I suggested soccer. And that's the only ball we could find."

To Ellie's amazement, they believed him. The Emperor nodded approvingly. "Soccer is a manly sport," he said.

"I'm surprised you can still walk," said the King. He stood on one foot, slipped off his other shoe, and rubbed his bruised, royal toes gently on the back of his leg.

A Surprise for Princess Ellie

"You'll find a much softer ball in the sports hall," suggested the Queen. She glanced at Ellie with a hint of suspicion in her eyes. "I'm surprised you didn't think of that yourself, Aurelia."

Ellie led John away quickly, before her mother had time to ask what they were really doing. It seemed safest to head in the direction of the sports hall and to get out of sight as soon as possible.

Suddenly, John stopped. "That's it!" he cried, pointing at a statue of an angel that stood on a ledge halfway up the wall.

"That's what?" asked Ellie.

The Pony-Crazed Princess

The statue had been there for as long as she could remember, and it looked exactly the same as it always had.

"The way into the secret passage, of course," said John. "I bet the statue is the lever that opens the door. That would explain why it's called the Angel Pathway."

"Should I pull it?" squealed Ellie, her eyes bright with excitement.

"No, I will!" said John. "I've got more experience with secret passages than you do." He reached up on tiptoe, took hold of the statue with both hands, and pulled the top of it down toward him.

The stone angel tipped slowly forward. Ellie glanced around, looking for a secret door. Then she looked back, just in time to see the angel overbalance and tumble off its

A Surprise for Princess Ellie

shelf. It landed on John's head, bounced off again and fell onto the floor.

"Ow," said John. "Is it all right?"

"I think so," said Ellie, peering at the top of his head. "I can't see any blood."

John pushed her away. "I meant the angel."

Ellie looked down and sighed with relief. The statue was still in one piece. John's head and the thick carpet had broken its fall. But there was no sign of a secret door. The statue wasn't a lever at all.

"Wrong again," said John, brightly. "So we should be right next time – third time is lucky."

"It's getting late. We'd better leave it till tomorrow," said Ellie. They had already had two disasters and she suspected it wasn't only *good* luck that came in threes.

But there was no chance of looking for secret passages the next morning. The palace was in turmoil as everyone prepared for the jubilee party. Maids were polishing the silver until it gleamed, footmen were putting up balloons, and gardeners were carrying in armfuls of flowers. No one wanted excited children getting in the way.

So Ellie and John put on their riding clothes, grabbed their backpacks, and retreated happily to the stable yard.

Kate was waiting for them with three

packed lunches. "My gran's made us these. She says we should stay out of everyone's way until the party starts."

"Let's go for a picnic ride," suggested Ellie. "I'll take Starlight." She knew she'd be less likely to worry about the bay mare if she could see her all the time.

"That's not a good idea," said Meg. "I don't think you should ride her until the vet has said she's all right."

Ellie's panic returned. "What's wrong with her?" she asked.

Meg smiled reassuringly. "Don't worry! I'm sure it's nothing serious. I've just got a suspicion, that's all. And if I'm right, you shouldn't be riding her."

"A suspicion of what?" asked Ellie.

"I'm not going to tell you," said Meg.

A Surprise for Princess Ellie

"I don't want you to be disappointed if I'm wrong."

Ellie looked at Meg in surprise. What was the matter with Starlight? she wondered. And why was Meg being so secretive about it?

Chapter 5

Ellie was still puzzling over Meg's words when they set out on the ride. But, gradually, the pleasure of riding Moonbeam pushed those thoughts to the back of her mind. She cantered across the deer park, with Kate and Rainbow on one side and John and Sundance on the other. Then they turned uphill into the woods, twisting and

turning between the trees until they came
out onto the open hilltop. They ate their
lunch there, overlooking the sea. It was
wonderful to be so far from the palace with
no one around except the ponies, and the
sheep that grazed on the heather.

"Let's go to the beach," suggested John,
as he gave his apple core to Sundance.

The Pony-Crazed Princess

"That would be great," said Kate. "But is there time before the party?"

"Of course there is," said Ellie. "We don't have to stay long."

The path down the cliff was steep and stony. The ponies' hooves slithered and slid on the pebbles as they picked their way down. Ellie was glad when they reached the beach and the stones stopped. Ahead of them lay a huge stretch of soft, white sand.

"Oh, the tide's out," said Kate, sounding disappointed. "The sea is so far away I can hardly see it."

"We can't paddle," moaned Ellie.

"But we *can* explore," said John. "We can ride out to that headland. We'd never be able to reach it at high tide."

Ellie looked in the direction he was

A Surprise for Princess Ellie

pointing and saw that he was right. On the other side of the beach, the cliff curved gracefully and headed toward the sea. It ended in a dramatic tumble of rocks. But there was no water around them today. The tide was so far out that the rocks were dry.

"Come on," called John. "There's sure to be all sorts of exciting things out there." He turned Sundance toward the headland and urged the chestnut pony into a gallop. Ellie and Kate raced after him. The ponies' tails streamed behind them in the wind, as their hooves pounded across the damp sand. Ellie leaned forward over Moonbeam's snow-white mane, enjoying the excitement of the gallop.

When they reached the headland, they slowed the ponies to a walk. "That was fantastic," said Ellie, as she patted the

palomino's neck. Then she spotted
something strange at the bottom of the cliff.
It was a huge, dark shape like a giant's mouth.

John had seen it too. He trotted
Sundance toward it and yelled, "It's a cave!"

Ellie and Kate followed him and peered
through the opening. The cave was even
larger than it looked from outside. They
couldn't see the back at all. The floor sloped
up gently from the entrance and
disappeared into the darkness.

"Let's explore,"
said John. He
urged Sundance
into the cave,
obviously
expecting the
others to follow.

A Surprise for Princess Ellie

"No!" said Kate, with a shudder. "It's scary. I don't want to go in there."

"Neither do I," said Ellie, happy that she wasn't the only one who was frightened.

"But we might find some hidden treasure," pleaded John from inside.

"Or something worse," said Kate. "Bats live in caves...and so do dragons."

John put his hand to his mouth and shouted, "Hello! Is anyone there?" His words echoed around the cave, bouncing back at him from the distant walls. But there was no other answer and no sound of scrabbling claws or flapping wings. "See. It's completely empty."

"I still don't want to go inside," said Ellie, firmly. "And I think you should come out." John looked so disappointed that, for a moment, she thought he might refuse. But his enthusiasm returned when she suggested looking for tide pools instead.

They found a sheltered patch of sand just outside the cave and tied the ponies to some nearby rocks. Then they left Moonbeam, Sundance and Rainbow to doze quietly in the sunshine, while the three of them set out to explore.

Soon, Ellie, John and Kate were clambering over the rocks, squealing with delight as they peered into the pools left behind by the tide. The water teemed with life – sea anemones, scuttling crabs and tiny fish that swam so fast they were hard to spot.

There was so much to see that they completely lost track of time. They moved

A Surprise for Princess Ellie

on from pool to pool, farther and farther
from the waiting ponies.

Finally, they reached a tall, arched rock
that marked the end of the headland.

"It's like a giant doorway," said Kate,
shading her eyes from the sun as she peered
up at it.

"Or a huge croquet hoop," giggled Ellie.

"Or an enormous cat flap," laughed John.

Suddenly, their laughter was cut short by a dreadful sound. It was the squeal of a terrified horse.

Chapter 6

Ellie whirled around and stared in horror. While they had been busy exploring, the tide had swept in, cutting off their route back to the shore. The low-lying sand they had cantered across was completely covered with water, and the three ponies were trapped against the cliff, huddled together in terror. Moonbeam squealed again, as another wave hit the rocks and soaked her with spray.

Ellie started to clamber back across the rocks. "We've got to save them!" she cried.

"And ourselves," added John, in a serious voice.

Ellie looked around and saw what he meant. The rocky headland was rapidly disappearing under the waves, too. "Of course," Ellie thought. "If there are tide pools it means the rocks must be submerged when the tide is in."

"Maybe we could swim to the beach," suggested John.

Ellie shook her head. "I don't think I can swim that far. I can only do two lengths of our pool. Although it is a very big pool," she added, defiantly.

A Surprise for Princess Ellie

"We could climb the arch," suggested Kate. "The top looks as if it never gets wet."

Ellie glanced up and saw that she was right. The arch could save them, but it couldn't save the ponies. Surely there was something else they could do?

Suddenly, Ellie had an idea. "We can take the ponies into the cave," she suggested. "We'll be safe in there."

"No!" cried Kate. "It'll fill up with water when the tide's right in."

"It won't," said John. "I know, because I've been inside. The floor slopes up, and tho ground at the back is completely dry. We'll be safe if we go far enough in."

Ellie shuddered as she remembered how scary the cave had looked. But she pushed away her fear and declared, "Come on!

It's the only way we can save the ponies."

They scrabbled over the rocks, retracing the route they had taken to reach the arch. But they were soon forced to give up. They couldn't get back the way they had come. Too many of the rocks were already underwater, and the waves that swept across the others threatened to knock them off their feet.

"We'll have to keep closer to the cliff," said John.

Ellie followed his advice and, to her relief, she found a ledge of rock just wide enough to stand on. It jutted out from the cliff face and was still a few inches above the water. The three children edged carefully along it, with their backs against the cliff. They held hands for extra balance and to give each other courage. Soon they were soaking wet

A Surprise for Princess Ellie

from the icy-cold spray of the waves. The wind blew through their wet clothes and whipped the waves even higher.

Ellie sighed with relief as they jumped down on the other side. Then they quickly untied the frightened ponies and led them into the shelter of the cave. "It's all right now," whispered Ellie, as she stroked Moonbeam's neck. "We're safe here."

The Pony-Crazed Princess

She smiled as she saw the terror fade from the pony's eyes. If only her own fear would disappear as easily.

A wave broke and washed into the cave, swishing gently around their feet. The children led the ponies further inside and found a good place to wait. It was close enough to the entrance to be in the light, but far enough back to be dry and safe.

"I wonder how long we'll have to stay here," said Kate, as they sat huddled together on the cold rock floor.

A Surprise for Princess Ellie

"Several hours, at least," said John. "It'll take that long for the tide to go out again."

"Maybe we should talk about something else to pass the time," suggested Ellie. "Did your dad call last night, Kate?"

Her friend nodded miserably. "I asked him again about a pony, but he still says 'no'. He just doesn't understand how much I want one."

"I'm sorry," said Ellie. She knew there was nothing she could say that would help Kate, so she decided to change the subject. She glanced at her watch and groaned dramatically. "We're going to miss the party. I'll be in big trouble when we get back."

"So will I," said John. Then he grinned. "But at least we won't have to sing that silly song."

The Pony-Crazed Princess

Kate looked confused. So John and Ellie explained about their rehearsal with Miss Stringle and, to pass the time, they taught her the song as well. Singing helped drown out the sound of the waves, and it kept their minds off the danger. So did loudly crunching the chips left over from lunch.

But, eventually, they ran out of things to do. Ellie and Kate sat in silence, staring dismally at the water and wishing it would go away. John was restless.

"I'm bored," he announced. "Let's explore."

Ellie eyed the darkness nervously and shook her head. "We can't – not without a light."

"I've got a flashlight in my survival kit," said John.

A Surprise for Princess Ellie

"Your what?" asked Kate.

"My survival kit," repeated John, as he pulled a plastic box from his backpack. "All good explorers have one. I learned about it on the internet."

Ellie was intrigued. She peered at the box and asked, "What's in it?"

John snapped open the lid proudly and pulled out the contents, one by one. "This is a piece of explorer-grade, extra-white, super-visible chalk," he explained. "This is a bar of explorer-grade, high-energy chocolate, specially designed to prevent starvation in tricky places. This is a ball of explorer-grade string – its super strength means it can lift an elephant out of a swamp without breaking."

"We don't need that," giggled Kate. "There aren't any elephants around here."

John ignored her. "And this is my flashlight."

"Explorer-grade?" asked Ellie.

"Nope," said John. "Just waterproof, shockproof and shatterproof." As he spoke, he switched it on and shone the beam of light around the cave.

Suddenly, he stopped and stared, his eyes wide with amazement. "Wow!" he yelled. "There's something there – right at the back of the cave."

Chapter 7

John ran into the darkness, taking the flashlight and Sundance with him. Moonbeam tried to follow but Ellie held her back. Although John had persuaded her that there wasn't a dragon, she could think of plenty of other monsters that might be lurking in the shadows.

"Come on," called John. "You must see this."

"Is it alive?" asked Ellie, nervously.

"No," said John.

"Are you sure?" said Kate.

"Of course I am," he replied, with growing impatience.

Ellie and Kate led their ponies cautiously toward the small patch of light. But there wasn't a monster. John had found the entrance to a long, dark tunnel.

Ellie's fear was immediately replaced by curiosity. "Where do you think it goes?" she asked.

"Let's find out," suggested John. "Now we've found a secret passage, we've got to go down it."

Ellie grinned. Exploring the tunnel sounded much more exciting than sitting in the cave with nothing to do. There was just

A Surprise for Princess Ellie

one problem. "What about the ponies? We can't leave them here alone."

"We'll take them with us," declared John. "The tunnel's too low to ride along but there's enough room to lead them."

Kate looked doubtful. "What if we get lost. I don't want to stay in there forever."

"That's why all good explorers need a piece of this," said John, pulling out the

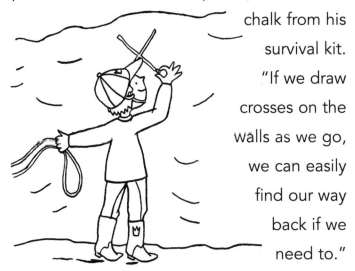

chalk from his survival kit. "If we draw crosses on the walls as we go, we can easily find our way back if we need to."

He led the way into the tunnel, leading Sundance behind him. The chestnut pony followed happily, with his ears pricked as if he were enjoying the adventure.

Moonbeam was less enthusiastic. She stared suspiciously at the hole in the wall and snorted through her nose. "There's nothing to be frightened of," whispered Ellie, as she stroked the pony's neck. The palomino relaxed a little and stepped slowly through the entrance. The tunnel was narrower than Ellie had expected, forcing her to stay close to Moonbeam's head. But she didn't mind. The warm, friendly scent of horse helped to mask the smell of the damp, stale air.

"Is this the Angel Pathway?" asked Kate, from her position at the back.

A Surprise for Princess Ellie

"It might be," said Ellie.

"But it might not," argued John. "I read on the internet that secret passages near the sea are usually made by pirates or smugglers. It didn't say anything about kings."

They walked in silence for a long time, pausing every few minutes while John chalked another cross on the wall. The farther they went, the more Ellie felt her initial enthusiasm disappear. She didn't like the narrow tunnel. She didn't like the echoing sound of their footsteps, and she didn't like the darkness that lay beyond the small patch of light from the flashlight.

"We should have been back at the stable yard by now," said Kate, eventually. "Do you think they'll be worried about us?"

John shone his flashlight on his watch

and shook his head. "Not yet. They'll just be upset because we're late. The party must have started."

"I wish we were there," sighed Ellie.

"I wish we were anywhere but here," groaned Kate. "My feet ache."

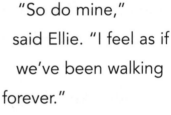

"So do mine," said Ellie. "I feel as if we've been walking forever."

"No," said John, as he looked at his watch again. "Only for seventeen and a half minutes."

Suddenly, Ellie noticed that the light wasn't as bright as

A Surprise for Princess Ellie

before. "What's wrong with the flashlight?" she asked in alarm.

John peered into the front of it and groaned. "I think the batteries are starting to go dead."

"Surely they should have lasted longer than that?" said Kate.

"Maybe you should have used explorer-grade ones," added Ellie.

John sighed. "Maybe I shouldn't have used it so much to make shadow pictures on my bedroom wall. Look – I can make a really good rabbit if I waggle my fingers like this."

Ellie was not impressed. She just wanted to get out of the tunnel before the flashlight stopped working. "Will it last long enough to get us back to the cave?" she asked.

"It should, if we hurry," said John. "Let's go."

Ellie tried to swing Moonbeam around to face the opposite way. But it was impossible. The tunnel was too narrow. There wasn't enough room for the ponies to turn. Ellie felt her stomach knot with fear. There was no way they could get back to the cave. They had to keep walking into the unknown, and soon they would be doing it in the dark.

Chapter 8

Ellie, John and Kate led the ponies along the tunnel as quickly as they could. They were desperate to find a way out, before the flashlight batteries went completely dead. Their fear grew as the light got dimmer and dimmer. This adventure wasn't fun anymore. It was too scary.

"What if there isn't a way out," cried

Kate. She sounded very close to tears.

"There must be," said John. "No one would build a secret passage that doesn't go anywhere."

Ellie hoped he was right. She didn't mention her fear that the tunnel might be blocked by fallen rocks. There was no point in upsetting Kate even more. Instead, she stared at the ground, concentrating on her feet and trying to forget about the closeness of the walls. As a result, she didn't notice that Sundance had stopped until she walked into his tail. The chestnut pony stamped his back foot in surprise and looked around to see what was happening.

"You can come past," called John. "It's wider here."

Ellie and Kate led their ponies up beside

A Surprise for Princess Ellie

him, while John shone the flashlight around the walls. "It's much too square to be a cave," he said. "It's some sort of secret room."

"I guess that's what you'd expect at the end of a secret passage," said Ellie.

"But there isn't a door," groaned Kate. "There's no way out. We're going to be trapped here forever."

"No, we're not," said John. "There's room to turn the ponies here so we can go back the way we came."

Ellie bit her lip nervously. The flashlight batteries were very nearly dead, and she hated the idea of walking all the way back in the dark. Surely there must be another solution. "Maybe there's a secret door," she suggested.

The Pony-Crazed Princess

John shone the flashlight around again. This time Ellie noticed that the wall at the far end was smoother than the others. She led Moonbeam over to it and ran her hands across its surface. "It's made of wood," she yelled, with a note of triumph in her voice. "Maybe the whole wall is one big door."

John and Kate led their ponies over to admire her discovery and all three of them started to search for a handle. At that moment, the flashlight went out completely, leaving them groping in the dark. Ellie's fingers closed on something smooth and round. She turned it as hard as she could and felt a wave of relief as she heard a loud click.

The wall swung slowly open, and light flooded in. It was dazzling after the darkness of the tunnel. Ellie closed her eyes for a moment to protect them. Then she opened them again and stared through the open doorway in surprise.

Ahead of her lay the Grand Ballroom of the palace. The jubilee party was in full swing, and the room was packed with people. The glittering light from the chandeliers made the ladies' diamond jewelry sparkle and the band's brass instruments gleam like gold.

The Pony-Crazed Princess

Maids ran this way and that carrying trays of sausages on sticks and tiny sandwiches, while gentle music mingled with the sound of many voices talking at once.

To Ellie's dismay, the sound rapidly died away. Conversations stopped. Even the band stopped playing. Everyone was staring at the mysterious opening in the wall and the strange, pony-shaped shadows lurking in the darkness.

Ellie spotted her parents just as they started to move toward the tunnel entrance. But she couldn't bear to wait for them to drag her out into the daylight. That would make her look like a naughty child in front of all these people. Worse still, it would probably ruin their party and

A Surprise for Princess Ellie

their special day. There must be something she could do to put things right, if only she could think of what it was.

Chapter 9

Ellie's mind raced as she searched for an answer. Then she had an idea. "Jump on quickly," she said. "There's only one thing we can do." She swung herself into Moonbeam's saddle and rode out through the opening, onto the small stage that stood in front of it. Then she smiled as brightly as she could and shouted, "Surprise, surprise!"

A Surprise for Princess Ellie

One of the maids was so shocked that she gave a small scream and dropped her sausages all over the floor. Everyone else was equally surprised, but much less clumsy. Their mouths dropped open in astonishment at the sight of three damp and dirty children riding through the ballroom wall on three equally damp and dirty ponies. They were even more amazed when they realized that two of the children were the Prince and Princess. Everyone stared at Ellie and her friends. No one moved at all, except the maid, who was desperately trying to pick up the sausages.

The Pony-Crazed Princess

"All together now," whispered Ellie. "On the count of three – one, two, three…" Luckily, Kate and John guessed what she wanted them to do. They joined in with her, singing Miss Stringle's song at the tops of their voices.

They sang all five verses perfectly. By the time they reached the end, the band had finally picked up the tune and joined in. So they sang the chorus once more with the music before they stopped. The guests broke into applause. Some of them even cheered.

A Surprise for Princess Ellie

Miss Stringle did neither. She looked rather faint and had to be helped to a chair, where she sat sipping water from a crystal glass and fanning herself with a serviette.

Great Aunt Edwina climbed onto the stage with amazing agility for a lady of her age. "You found it!" she cried in great excitement.

"What do you mean?" asked Ellie.

"The Angel Pathway, of course." She peered into the tunnel entrance and added, "We never found that when I was a girl."

Ellie looked back at the secret door they had come through. On this side, it was disguised as an enormous painting of angels. Suddenly everything made sense. It was the picture that gave the tunnel its name.

The guests clapped their hands again

as the King and Queen stepped onto the
stage. The King raised his arms and waited
for silence. Then he announced, "I'm sure
we are all delighted with my daughter's
surprise entertainment. Now please continue
with the festivities and enjoy yourselves."
He waved at the band to start playing again,
and the guests went back to eating, talking
and dancing.

The Queen smiled at Ellie and her
friends. "That was a lovely song, and a real
surprise."

"It was certainly unexpected," added the
King. He glanced over to Miss Stringle, who
still hadn't quite recovered from the shock.
"I think maybe it wasn't quite as it was
planned, but everything seems to have
worked out all right in the end."

A Surprise for Princess Ellie

At that moment, there was a commotion by the door. Meg rushed in, wearing her stable clothes and looking nearly as out of place as the children among the beautifully dressed guests. She looked relieved when she saw Ellie. "Thank goodness you're here. I've been getting really worried about you." Then she stopped and scratched her head thoughtfully. "But how did you get the ponies inside?"

"That's a very good question," said the King. "But more to the point, how do you plan to get them out again?"

Ellie hadn't thought of that. Fortunately John had. "We can go through those," he said, pointing across the ballroom to the French windows that led into the garden.

"And I suggest you do it as soon as possible," said the Queen. She smiled at a footman who had just arrived with a bucket and a shovel. "I don't think your ponies are house-trained."

A Surprise for Princess Ellie

Meg grinned. "There's another good reason for hurrying, but I'm not going to tell you what it is. You'll have to come back to the stable yard and see for yourselves. I want it to be a surprise."

Chapter 10

Ellie and John and Kate rode the ponies across the ballroom and out through the French windows, closely followed by the footman with the bucket and another with a mop to clean up the drips and wet hoofprints. Then they trotted to the stable yard as quickly as they could. They wanted to see the surprise right away, but Meg made them wait until they had unsaddled Sundance, Moonbeam and Rainbow and settled them in their stalls.

Then she led them across the stable yard and put her finger to her lips as she opened Starlight's door. The bay mare whickered to them as they peered inside. But, to their amazement, she wasn't alone. Nestled in the straw was a beautiful newborn foal.

"Wow!" said John and Kate together, their eyes wide with delight.

The Pony-Crazed Princess

"He's gorgeous," said Ellie. She had never seen anything as wonderful in her whole life.

"He's a she actually," explained Meg. "And she came much sooner than I expected. I'd guessed Starlight was in foal, but I wasn't going to tell you until I'd checked with the vet."

"I've been so worried about her," laughed Ellie. "But now everything is absolutely perfect." She had fallen instantly in love with the foal and couldn't stop looking at her. She wasn't a bay like her mother. She was a skewbald with pretty patches of brown and white hair. Her short mane stood straight up like a brush and her tail was short and stubby.

Starlight whickered again and nuzzled her new baby. The foal responded by pushing

A Surprise for Princess Ellie

on the ground with her spindly front legs and trying to stand. It didn't work. When she was only halfway up, she lost her balance and tumbled onto her side.

"Oh, no!" gasped Ellie. "Is she hurt?"

Meg shook her head. "Don't worry. She'll be fine."

"Should we help?" asked Kate, anxiously. "Her legs are so long, she doesn't know what to do with them."

"Give her time," said Meg. "She'll learn. She just needs some practice."

They all held their breath as the foal tried again. This time, she managed to get her front legs straight. It was the back ones that caused the trouble. When they were only halfway up, she slipped forward onto her knees. She rested for a moment, kneeling in the straw. Then she pushed up with her front hooves again, and everyone gave a sigh of relief as she finally managed to stand.

Starlight proudly guided her baby's wobbly steps until the foal was standing close beside her.

"What are you going to call her?" asked the Queen.

Ellie jumped at the sound of her mother's voice. She had been so engrossed in the

A Surprise for Princess Ellie

foal that she hadn't noticed her parents arrive. They both looked very happy.

"What a surprise!" said the King, as he put his arm around Ellie's shoulder. "You are a lucky girl. Imagine having six ponies."

Suddenly, Ellie thought of something. "I've got a brilliant idea," she whispered. "I want you both to come outside so I can tell you."

The King's face fell as he followed her into the stable yard. "Your ideas usually mean trouble, Aurelia." But, as he listened to Ellie whispering in his ear, he started to smile.

Then he whispered in the Queen's ear, and she smiled too. "For once I agree with you," said the King. "This time you really have thought of a *brilliant* idea."

"So you don't mind?" asked Ellie.

"Not even a tiny bit," said the Queen. She gave Ellie a gentle kiss. "In fact, I'm proud of you for thinking of it."

When they went back into the stable yard, they found Kate stroking the foal's brown and white neck. "Isn't she sweet?" she said. "She's a real angel."

"That would be a good name," said Ellie. "Angel would suit her."

"And it would remind us of our adventure," said John.

"But Jubilee would remind us all of the day she was born," suggested the Queen.

A Surprise for Princess Ellie

"And Comet would fit in with your other ponies," said the King. "They all have names to do with the sky."

"It sounds as if you've narrowed the choice down to three," said Meg. "Which is it going to be – Jubilee, Angel or Comet? The choice is yours, Ellie."

"No, it's not," said Ellie. "It's up to Kate."

Kate looked up in surprise. "Why me?" she asked.

"Because she's your pony," said Ellie. "I want you to have her."

Kate's surprise turned to astonishment. "You can't mean that."

"Yes, I can," said Ellie, firmly.

Kate ran over and hugged Ellie. "You must be the best friend in the whole world."

The Pony-Crazed Princess

"So are you," said Ellie, as she hugged her back.

John sighed. "This lovey-dovey stuff is all very well, but we still don't know the foal's name."

"She's Angel," said Kate. "My Angel."

"Forever and ever," said Ellie.

If you've enjoyed The Pony-Crazed Princess,
you might also enjoy:

Amy Wild, Animal Talker

by Diana Kimpton

Welcome to the world of Amy Wild, where dogs
tell their secrets, cats perform rescue missions,
and an entire island is squeaking and squawking
with animal magic!